The Legend of

WILLIAM
TELL

To Frederick Small, whose son I am;
To Sandy and Catlin, whose father I am.
—T.S.

THE LEGEND OF WILLIAM TELL

A Bantam Little Rooster Book / April 1991

*Little Rooster is a trademark of Bantam Books, a division of
Bantam Doubleday Dell Publishing Group, Inc.*

*All rights reserved.
Text and illustrations copyright © 1991 by Terry Small.*

Designed by GDS / Jeffrey L. Ward

*No part of this book may be reproduced or transmitted
in any form or by any means, electronic or mechanical,
including photocopying, recording, or by any information
storage and retrieval system, without permission in
writing from the publisher.
For information address: Bantam Books.*

Library of Congress Cataloging-in-Publication Data
Small, Terry.
   The legend of William Tell / by Terry Small.
      p.   cm.
   "A Bantam little rooster book."
   Summary: Recounts in rhyme the story of the legendary Swiss folk
hero who shot the apple from his son's head.
   ISBN 0-553-07031-2
   1. Tell, Wilhelm—Legends.   [1. Tell, William—Legends.
2. Folklore—Switzerland.   3. Stories in rhyme.]   I. Title.
PZ8.3.S63537Le   1991
398.22'09494—dc20   89-18548
[E]   CIP
                                                                      AC

Published simultaneously in the United States and Canada

*Bantam Books are published by Bantam Books, a division of Bantam Doubleday
Dell Publishing Group, Inc. Its trademark, consisting of the words "Bantam
Books" and the portrayal of a rooster, is Registered in U.S. Patent and Trademark
Office and in other countries. Marca Registrada. Bantam Books, 666 Fifth Avenue,
New York, New York 10103.*

PRINTED IN HONG KONG

0 9 8 7 6 5 4 3 2 1

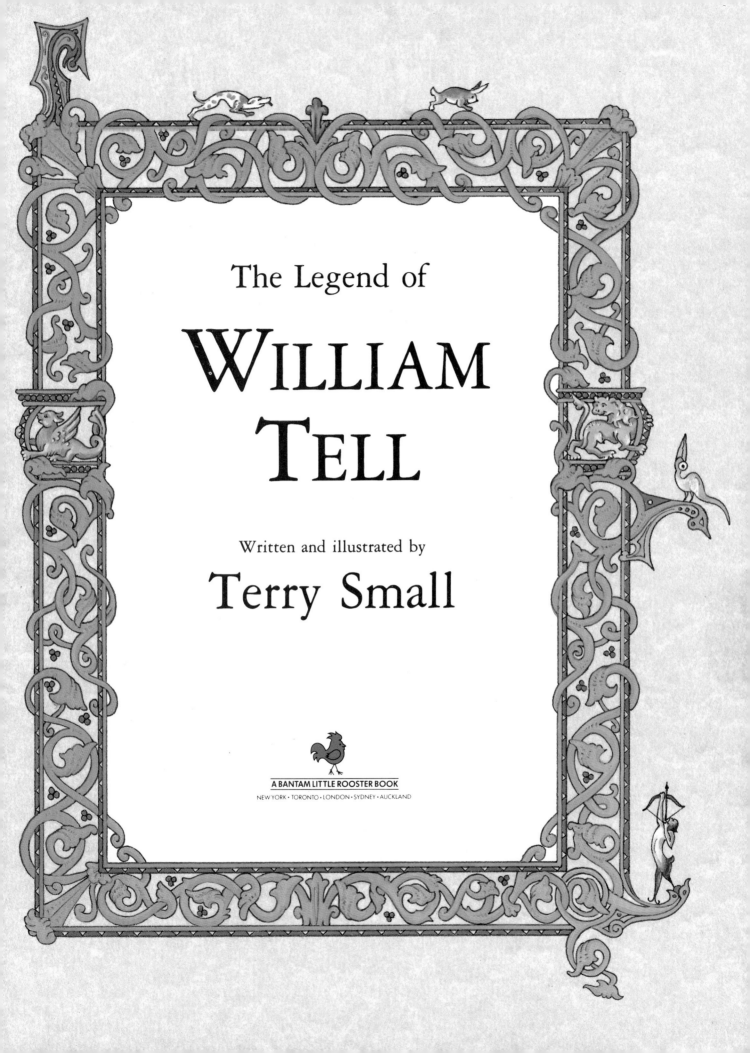

The Legend of

WILLIAM TELL

Written and illustrated by

Terry Small

A BANTAM LITTLE ROOSTER BOOK
NEW YORK · TORONTO · LONDON · SYDNEY · AUCKLAND

There's a land where the mountains plunge to the lakes
And the rivers run deep and wild,
And the pines reach up where the ice creeps down
To the place where Fortune smiled.

It's a land of forest, sun, and snow,
Where the winters are harsh and stern;
But the summers are bliss in the land of the Swiss
By the shores of Lake Lucerne.

As proud as the pine, as free as the wind
Were the men of that savage slope
Till they suffered the sword of the Austrian lord
And surrendered their freedom and hope.

A viceroy came from a foreign land
And occupied Altdorf plain;
And the people's pride was buried inside
At the time of the tyrant's reign.

With a fist of iron and a heart of stone
And the Empire at his back,
His name was a hiss on the tongues of the Swiss:
Gessler! Gessler the Black!

"I should have been lord of a civilized state
With cathedrals and plazas and fountains;
But I gambled the whole on an ill-fated roll:
The dice sent me into these mountains!

"But what Gessler wins, Gessler keeps.
My power is absolute!
You'll serve my men or I'll teach you again
Respect for the heel of my boot!"

Then Gessler kicked at the carpenter's son
And knocked him flat on the ground.
"Let him lie in the dirt! He deserves to be hurt!
While I spoke he was glancing around!"

Then off he rode with his guard behind
And the people were left to tremble;
And the order came down to the center of town:
No crowd is allowed to assemble.

In nervous whispers people spoke
In groups of twos and threes,
While soldiers posted daily
Gessler's list of new decrees.

A widow drawn to touch his hem
Was dragged from the viceroy's path:
"Who dares to stroke the viceroy's cloak
Shall feel the viceroy's wrath!"

A lad who smelled of the flocks he drove
Was beaten in public view:
"Those who keep their goats and sheep
Must keep their distance, too!"

A thatcher working on a roof
Was cast in a dungeon dire:
"When I approach by horse or coach
Let none be seated higher."

And so it went for weeks and months:
"Don't speak of the happy past;
Don't laugh too loud; don't look too proud;
Don't stand on the shadow I cast!"

But men who feared to look at his face
Stared daggers at his back;
And hearts would flame when they spoke the name
Of Gessler—Gessler the Black!

When November came to the Altdorf plain
Crisp and bright and dry,
The guards were there in the village square
Raising a pole on high.

Then Gessler's hat was placed on top
Like bait in a hunter's trap;
And every soul who passed that pole
Was ordered to kneel to the cap.

"Kneel to a cap!" the Swiss exclaimed,
And the guards replied to a few,
"It's kneel as planned or lose your land,
Your flocks and families, too.

"It's kneel to the cap or taste the lash,
Or rot in a prison hole;
And just be glad it's only a cap
And not your head on a pole!"

"Kneel to a cap?" echoed the Swiss.
"Never!" they silently vowed,
And they stayed away that November day
And held their heads unbowed.

Week upon week in the marketplace
That cap hung in the air
While an armed patrol stood round the pole
And guarded an empty square.

No one bought and no one sold
And no one came or went;
No one's will was broken
And no one's knee was bent.

Some miles away a woodsman roamed—
Near Burglen did he dwell.
In hunting deer he had no peer,
And his name was William Tell.

True he was to the cross he wore,
So said the folks who knew him,
But truer still to the crossbow skill
That God had given to him.

He'd shot an apple out of a tree
The one time that he'd tried;
But rumor claimed he'd really aimed
And hit the worm inside.

One morning early, Tell set out
With his young son at his side.
"Come with me down to Altdorf town
Where friends of mine reside.

"For I've been too long in these wooded hills
A-chasing the hart and the hind;
Farewell to the roe; we'll hunt down below
For hearts of a different kind."

But when they arrived in the center of town
They were shocked by the sight before them:
With time to waste, some soldiers paced
At a job that seemed to bore them.

High overhead on a lofty pole
Was a cap that flapped in the breeze;
And they heard a cry from a guard nearby,
"Halt there! Down on your knees!"

"Down on my knees?" bold Tell replied.
"You joke, but I don't laugh.
My knee never bends to the dearest of friends,
Much less to a stranger's staff!"

"No stranger, he," the soldier said,
"But your very lord and master.
His staff will crack your insolent back
If you don't obey any faster!"

Tell turned away but the soldier's halberd
Stopped him with a poke.
"Stay awhile—perhaps you'll smile
When Gessler tells the joke."

A horn was blown and all at once
The dreaded Gessler came,
"How dare you teach your boy to breach
The law that I proclaim!

"Bend your back and sniff the dirt
And honor Gessler's cap!
Or those sturdy knees I'll chop like trees
And your blood will run like sap!"

"I'd never bow to an empty cap
Nor yet to the man who fills it.
My blood runs free inside of me
And woe to the man who spills it."

Then Gessler snarled at Tell's reply,
Reached out and grabbed his son.
"We'll see how free your blood will be
When Gessler's work is done!"

"Release the lad!" his father cried,
"We'll both be on our way.
For William Tell and his son know well
Which Master to obey!"

"Ah, William Tell—I've heard the name
Pronounced in epic terms:
A country Swiss who'd never miss
A chance to shoot at worms!"

He dragged the boy to an apple tree
And stood him between the roots.
"I've picked you for a target," he said.
"*You* pick the one who shoots."

The boy replied, "All marksmen know
That only one excels.
No truer bow do these mountains know
Than my father's, William Tell's."

Then Gessler laughed and shook his head.
"Your choice is worse than his!
For now, I trust, we'll find out just
How good he really is.

"Now, here's an apple for his bow—
I'll prop it on your head;
And if he aims a little low
He'll shoot his son instead."

That mighty blast of the soldier's horn,
Which had called the viceroy there,
Had summoned as well the friends of Tell,
Who gathered in the square.

They watched as William Tell was seized.
They saw him dragged and shoved.
And they heard him cry he would rather die
Than shoot at the one he loved.

But Gessler smiled a wicked smile
As only Gessler could.
"If you won't shoot your favorite fruit,
I'm sure my soldiers would."

Then William Tell, to spare a life,
Agreed to press his skill.
"One single arrow," Gessler said,
"To do the devil's will.

"One single arrow—choose it well—
One arrow and one shot.
It just takes one if it's skillfully done,
And it just takes one if it's not."

Then Tell spun around to look in his quiver
While turning his back on the rest;
And after he tried all the arrows inside
He quietly pulled out the best.

"A hundred paces," Gessler added.
"No! A hundred and one!
I'll bet my purse it'll be no worse
For the apple than for the son."

Tell walked back to that distant spot
And knelt with crossbow ready.
He called on his skill, for his heart to be still,
His hand and his eye to be steady.

He whispered low, "I call on the God
Who marks the fall of the sparrow
And numbers the hairs of my own son's head
To guide the flight of my arrow."

And then he squeezed the crossbow's trigger
That let the arrow fly:
The tree was hit, the apple split
And fell to the earth nearby.

A shout went up—a mighty shout
From the Swiss who filled the square!
And they watched Tell run to embrace his son
In the cool November air.

"William Tell!" they began to yell
In a crowd by law forbidden.
But their shouting stopped as an arrow dropped
From his shirt where it had been hidden.

"What's this? An arrow?" Gessler cried.
"An arrow feathered in red?
I said one shot was all you got,
But you planned for two instead!"

"The first was for the apple
That I had to split apart;
But if I'd hit my boy with it,
The next was for your heart!"

"Seize the traitor!" Gessler raged,
"We'll see how bravely he dies!"
But the voice of the crowd, united and proud,
Took the viceroy by surprise:

"Down with the cap! Down with the pole!
And down with Gessler, too!"
Then the crowd arose and came to blows
As passions stirred anew.

History tells of the Swiss revolt
By the shores of Lake Lucerne,
Of the patriots' call and the tyrant's fall
And of freedom's brave return.

But legend adds that hope was dim
Till Gessler the Black lay dead—
Till liberty came with the deadly aim
Of an arrow feathered in red.

And now in the land of mountain lakes
There's a magic that weaves its spell,
And a peace endures that forever ensures
The fame of William Tell!